This book b

Children's
POOLBEG

First published 1989 by
Poolbeg Press Ltd.
Knocksedan House,
Swords, Co. Dublin, Ireland.

Reprinted 1991

© Tony Hickey 1989

This book is published with the assistance of
The Arts Council/An Chomhairle Ealaíon, Ireland.

ISBN 1 85371 043 1

Cover design by Steven Hope
Illustrated by Steven Hope
Typeset by Print-Forme,
62 Santry Close, Dublin 9.
Printed by The Guernsey Press Ltd.,
Vale, Guernsey, Channel Islands.

Maeve Keaveney

Blanketland

maeve keaveney

Blanketland

Tony Hickey

Children's
POOLBEG

A Book to Read and Colour Yourself*

* The use of crayons or coloured pencils is recommended

Contents

The Land of Blankets

...ian the Leprechaun ...wned the smallest ...travel agency in the world. It was situated at the foot of the biggest oak tree in the wood.

It was so small that only other leprechauns and the wild creatures of the wood knew that it was there.

Brian and the wild creatures were the very best of friends. Without the help of the wild creatures Brian could not have run his travel agency.

They helped his customers to travel from one place to another.

The foxes and the badgers carried travelling leprechauns across the countryside.

1

The Land of Blankets

rian the Leprechaun owned the smallest travel agency in the world. It was situated at the foot of the biggest oak tree in the wood.

It was so small that only other leprechauns and the wild creatures of the wood knew that it was there.

Brian and the wild creatures were the very best of friends. Without the help of the wild creatures Brian could not have run his travel agency.

They helped his customers to travel from one place to another.

The foxes and the badgers carried travelling leprechauns across the countryside.

The birds took travelling leprechauns on longer journeys, sometimes as far as the sea.

From there the seagulls would carry the travelling leprechauns to visit their aunts and uncles and cousins in places far far away.

One fine morning, as Brian was eating his breakfast, Bríd the blackbird tapped on the kitchen window.

Brian opened the window and said "Hello, Bríd. What brings you around here so early in the day?"

"My favourite human is not well," Bríd said.

"Dear oh dear," said Brian. "I'm sorry to hear that. Who is your favourite human?"

"My favourite human is Paul," Bríd said. "His parents own the farm next to the big green hill. He never forgets to put out food for us birds in the cold weather. When I called at the farm just now I heard his mother say 'Poor Paul has a terrible cold. I think he had better stay in bed for a few days.' Paul is now very sad."

"How odd," said Brian. "I'd have

thought that Paul would be glad not to have to go to school."

"Paul loves school," Bríd said. "He has friends to play with there. But there are no children living anywhere near the farm."

"So he is feeling very lonely," Brian said.

"That's right," said Bríd. "Please come with me and try and cheer him up.

"Well, I'll do my best," said Brian. "But you will have to take me to the farm."

"Of course I'll do that" said Bríd.

Brian put on his warmest jacket and wound his longest scarf around his neck. Flying on such a frosty morning could be quite chilly.

Bríd carried Brian out of the wood and high up over the countryside.

Soon they reached the big green hill.

Next to the big green hill was the farmhouse where Paul lived.

Bríd landed on the window ledge of Paul's bedroom.

Brian looked in through the window. He saw Paul in bed.

Paul was all covered up with blankets

and looked very sad and lonely.

"How am I going to get inside?" Brian asked Bríd.

"The bathroom window is always left open," Bríd said. "I can take you around there."

A few seconds later Brian was inside the bathroom. He ran out onto the landing.

Fortunately the door to Paul's bedroom had been left open in case he needed to call downstairs to his mother.

Brian climbed up onto Paul's bed. "Hello, Paul," he said.

Paul's eyes opened in amazement. "Who are you?" he asked.

"I'm Brian the Leprechaun. I own a travel agency," Brian said.

"I thought leprechauns mended shoes and boots," Paul said.

"Some of us still do," said Brian. "But some of us do other jobs as well. I've come to cheer you up."

"Nothing can cheer me up," said Paul. "I feel terrible. And I'm missing a great game of chasing at school."

"How would it be if we went on a journey?" asked Brian. "After all, I am a travel agent."

"A journey?" Paul's eyes opened even further. "If I'm too sick to go to school how can I go on a journey?"

"That's easy," said Brian. "We'll go on a journey to Blanketland."

"I've never heard of Blanketland," said Paul "Where is it?"

"Here in front of your eyes," Brian said and pointed to the creases and folds in the bedclothes. "There is what looks like a valley. There is what looks like a lake. There is what looks like a forest on the side of a hill."

"You're right," said Paul. "The creases and folds in the bedclothes do look like a valley and a road and a lake and a forest on the side of a hill. But how do we get to Blanketland?"

"We just close our eyes, count to three and pretend that we are jumping," said Brian. "Are you ready."

Paul closed his eyes. "Yes," he said "I'm ready."

He heard Brian very slowly count. "One, two, three."

Then he pretended to jump.

When he opened his eyes he was standing on a road next to a lake.

In front of him was a hill with a forest on it.

All around him was the loveliest green grass he had ever seen.

He touched the grass. It was warm and soft and quite different from the grass that grew on the farm.

All the trees and hedges seemed to be the same as the grass.

He looked at Brian, who was standing beside him.

Brian's eyes twinkled with laughter. "Have you not guessed yet why everything in Blanketland is so different?" asked Brian.

"Do you mean because it's all made from blankets?" asked Paul.

"That is exactly what I mean," said Brian.

"And so it isn't real water in the lake?" Paul dipped his hand in the lake. It felt warm and dry like the grass.

At that moment a very strange coach pulled by two very strange looking horses came around a bend in the road.

The coach rocked from side to side.

The legs of the horse were wobbling.

The coachman was bounced around on his seat.

Then suddenly the coach seemed to jump up in the air.

The coachman was thrown off and landed on top of the lake.

The horses fell into the ditch.

The coach spun around several times in the middle of road. Its wheels fell off. It fell on its side.

A very fat man and a very fat woman climbed out of the wrecked coach. They wore very old-fashioned clothes. They were both very angry. They began to speak in very cross voices.

"It's a disgrace," the woman said.

"It's a shame," said the man. "Now we are going to be late for the circus."

"The circus!" said Paul "Are you in the circus?"

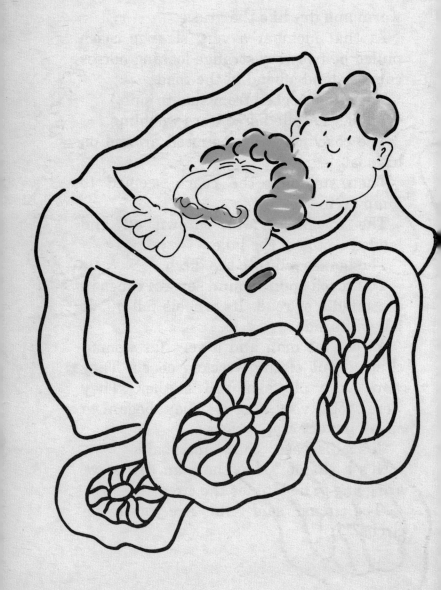

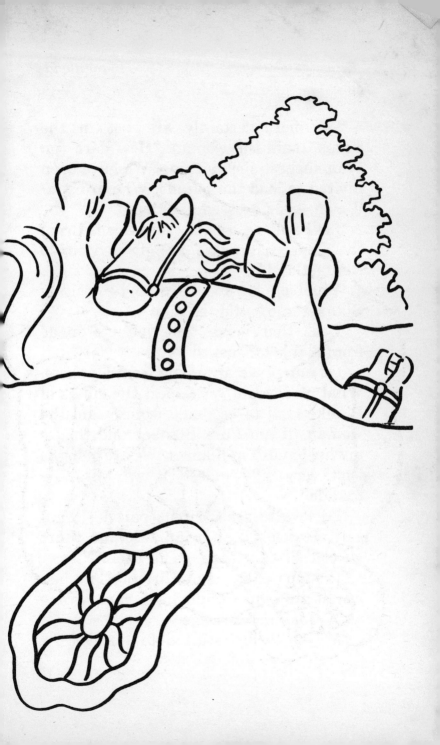

"We most certainly are not in the circus," said the woman. "How dare you even suggest such a thing! We have been invited to lead the parade. Who are you? Why are you dressed like that?"

"I'm Paul," said Paul. "And this is Brian the Leprechaun. We are on a visit to Blanketland."

"You look far too hard to be visiting Blanketland," said the man.

"Does that mean that you are made from blankets?" asked Paul.

"Of course we are made from blankets. What else would you expect the rulers of Blanketland to be made from?" said the woman. "I am Pure Blanket and this is my husband, Top Blanket. We are going to look very silly indeed if we miss the parade."

"I'd love to see a circus parade," Paul said. He looked at Brian. "Do you think we could fix the carriage for them?"

"I suppose so," said Brian. "I'm just wondering what could have gone wrong with a blanket carriage."

"Maybe it has started to unravel for

some reason," Paul said. "We had a blanket at home that unravelled so much that we made it into a bed for the dog."

"Well, I hope you aren't suggesting that we turn our lovely new carriage into a dog's bed," said Top Blanket.

"We had it made specially to lead the circus parade," said Pure Blanket.

"Oh no, we weren't suggesting that at all," said Brian. "Is it alright if Paul and I examine the carriage?"

"Yes, as long as you are very quick about it," said Top Blanket.

Brian and Paul gathered the pieces of the carriage together. Since they were made of blankets they were very easy to lift. Fitting them back together was like doing a huge jigsaw.

"You try and hold them in place," said Brian, "while I have a look underneath."

Brian looked under the carriage. A long thread was hanging down, almost touching the road.

"You were right," Brian said to Paul. "It is starting to unravel."

"Can you fix it?" Paul asked, managing

somehow to keep the pieces of the carriage together.

"Of course I can," said Brian. "All leprechauns carry a needle and thread in case they come across a pair of shoes or boots that need mending. I have mine with me."

Very carefully, Brian stitched the loose thread back into place. Then he put some new stitches around the wheels.

"There you are," he said. "The carriage is as good as new."

The coachman ran across the lake and led the horses out of the ditch. He put them back between the shafts of the coach, fixed their harness and jumped back onto his seat.

"Ready when you are," he said to Mr and Mrs Blanket.

"You've both been very helpful," Top Blanket said to Brian and Paul. "As a reward you may come to the parade and the circus with us."

Paul and Brian got into the carriage beside the Blankets and set off on a very strange journey.

The carriage still wobbled but not as much as before. What made the journey so odd was the way the trees and the hedges bobbed up and down as the carriage passed.

"It's the extra weight of you two hard creatures that makes that happen," Pure Blanket explained.

In the distance there were huge white mountains. Paul was sure he had seen them somewhere before.

"What are those mountains called?" he asked.

"Those are the Pillow Mountains," Top Blanket replied.

"They look just like the pillows on my bed," Paul whispered to Brian.

"That's exactly what they are," Brian whispered back.

The carriage came to the main street of a big town..

The circus parade was waiting at the top of the street. There was a blanket band to lead the parade. There were clowns and acrobats and animals of all kinds.

"Let the big parade begin," said Top Blanket.

"And please remember to wave," Pure Blanket said to Paul and Brian. "The people expect you to."

Brian and Paul leaned out the windows on their side of the carriage and waved.

The people watching the circus parade all cheered and laughed and waved back.

At last the parade arrived at the tent, which was also made of blankets and was enormous.

Brian and Paul were given the seats next to the Blankets. "We should be able to see everything from here," said Brian.

The circus began. It was as strange as everything else in Blanketland. The blanket band played but the sound it made was so soft that it was very hard to hear the music. Clowns fell around the place and made soft thudding noises.

Lions opened their mouths wide but the sound they made was more like a group of kittens asking for milk.

Strangest of all were the blanket seals who wobbled like jelly when they tried to balance blanket balls on their noses.

But, apart from Paul and Brian, no one else seemed to think it at all odd. They all cheered loudly when the circus was over.

"Where are you going to now?" Top Blanket asked Paul and Brian.

"I'd like to visit the Pillow Mountains," said Paul.

"Well you'd better start immediately if you want to get there before dark," Pure Blanket said.

"We'll leave right now. And thank you for everything," Paul said. Then he ran out of the town with Brian running after him.

2

The Road to Pillow Mountains

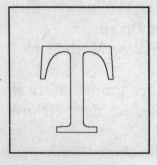 hey had gone only a very short distance when they had to sit down and rest.

"I don't know why I feel so tired," said Paul. "When I'm at home I can run four times as far and not even be out of breath."

"It's the blankets," said Brian. "They are so soft that every time we step on them they crease. We aren't able to run in a straight line. We keep going sideways."

"That's true," said Paul. "Even the edge of the road that we are sitting on is as soft as a jelly. And yet although we've only come a short distance we can no longer see the town where the circus is."

"I think that's because we are so heavy," said Brian. "We make such huge creases in the countryside that the town is now in a deep, deep valley."

"How amazing," said Paul. "We are changing the landscape just like it happened in the ice age."

"What's the landscape?" asked Brian.

"Oh it's all the things around us; the trees and the rivers and the fields and the mountains."

"And what was the ice age?"

"It was like the longest coldest winter you can imagine," said Paul, feeling very proud at being able to explain something to so wise a leprechaun as Brian. "It lasted for hundreds and hundreds of years. Everything was covered with ice. When the ice melted and started to move, it made all kinds of valleys and hills."

"I don't think I care very much for the sound of that." Brian shivered as he spoke. "It's not going to happen again, is it?"

"Not as far as I know," said Paul.

"Well I'm very glad to hear that," said

Brian. "Ordinary winters are bad enough. Now maybe we should go on our way again."

"All right," said Paul. "This time maybe we should walk more gently. That way we might not make so many creases."

"That's a very good idea," said Brian.

And so the two of them started down the road again, running almost on tip-toe.

The hedges and the trees along the sides of the road hardly moved at all as they hurried by.

But before very long they had to rest again.

"It's just as tiring running on tip-toe as it is going sideways," said Paul. "And we don't seem to be getting any closer to the mountains."

"That's true," said Brian. "But that often happens on a long journey. At first you seem to have gone only a very short distance. Then suddenly you are almost at the place."

"Yes but don't forget that Pure Blanket said that if we didn't leave at once we wouldn't get to the Pillow Mountains before dark. It's only the middle of the day now. Look at how bright the sun is."

Brian looked at the sun shining down out of the blue sky. "You are right," he said. "We might have to spend the entire afternoon running. We'll be worn out by the time we get there."

"I wish another carriage would come along," said Paul.

"Listen," said Brian. "I think I hear something right now."

Paul listened. He could hear a sound but he knew it couldn't be another carriage. Carriages in Blanketland made no sound. And, even if they did, it could never be a sound like the one he and Brian were listening to now.

"Whatever can it be?" asked Brian.

"I don't know, but it's certainly not a carriage," said Paul. "It's coming from the direction of the town."

At that very moment a herd of cows came over the top of the largest crease in the road. But they were quite different to any cows that Paul had ever seen before.

Instead of being black or white or grey

or brown these cows were bright blue and pale green and red. Some of them were even striped in a mixture of colours.

Even more strange than their colours was the way that they ran. Instead of moving two legs at a time the way ordinary cows run, they lifted all four off the ground at the same time. In fact they seemed to be bouncing rather than running.

They were also all exactly the same size and all their tails had exactly the same kind of curl.

The noise that Paul and Brian had heard came from the cows' mouths. Every time they touched the road they all cried "Klim! Klim!"

"What on earth is klim?" asked Brian.

"I know," said Paul "It's milk spelled backwards."

"But these cows aren't running backwards," said Brian.

"I know," said Paul. "But I don't think they are real cows."

"What are they then?" asked Brian.

"I think they are milk jugs. My granny

has a collection of jugs that is very old. Some of them look exactly like these cows. Even the colours are the same."

"But where are they going to?"

"They are going somewhere to be filled," said Paul. "That means there has to be a farm or a creamery somewhere further on. Come on. Let's follow them."

Brain and Paul began to run alongside the cows.

The cows paid no attention to them.

Brian leaned out and touched one of them.

"You're right, Paul," he said. "They are jugs. They are made of china."

"And the reason they bounce," Paul called out, for it was hard to be heard above the noise of 'klim, klim, klim,' "is that the blanket roads are very springy. It's like being on a trampoline. I'm going to try bouncing as well."

Paul jumped in the air and landed on the road.

The road made him bounce back up in the air.

"It's terrific," laughed Paul.

Brian tried it and agreed. "Yes. It is terrific and much easier than walking or running."

And so Brian and Paul and the herd of china cows bounced merrily down the road, leaving dozens of creases behind them.

"Have you noticed that not one of the cows has even the smallest chip out of it?" said Paul.

"That's because everything around is made of blanket," said Brian. "There is nothing hard for them to bang into."

"I wonder who they belong to," said Paul.

"I think we are going to find that out very soon," said Brian. "Read what's written on that sign."

Paul read the sign out loud. "'Welcome to Feather Farm. Bed and Breakfast. Afternoon Tea Served'."

Underneath the words an arrow pointed towards an open gate and a narrow winding road.

The cows began to bounce down this road.

"We might as well follow them," said Brian. "We can ask the farmer how far it is to the Pillow Mountains."

3

Feather Farm

 t's a funny name for a farm," said Paul.

"Not in Blanketland," said Brian. "After all what are most pillows made of?"

"Feathers," said Paul "Oh, and look, if they weren't green, I'd say that there were feathers growing in that field."

"I think they are feathers," said Brian.

"But feathers grow on birds," said Paul "not in fields."

"Maybe they've discovered a new way," said Brian. "After all, birds in Blanketland would be made of wool. They wouldn't have real feathers."

"Then why aren't the cows made of wool?" asked Paul.

32

"Because," said Brian "if they were made of wool you couldn't keep milk in them. It would leak out all over the place."

"But when the blanket people drink the milk would it not leak out all over them as well?" said Paul.

"I hadn't thought of that," said Brian. "We must ask the farmer. There he is coming out of that shed."

Brian pointed to a bright yellow and green shed that they could just see around a bend in the road. Coming out of it was a very tall man dressed in dark blue overalls. On his head he had a huge straw hat.

A short distance away from the shed there was a farmhouse with trees and a very pretty garden all around.

Paul and Brian and the cows bounced to a stop when they reached the tall man.

"Good day to you," said the tall man, politely raising his straw hat. "I'm Fred Feathers of Feather Farm. And here comes my wife, Freda Feathers."

Out of the house came a plump rosy-

cheeked woman in a pale pink dress. "Good day to you," she said. "Have you come for afternoon tea or are you looking for bed and breakfast?"

"Neither as a matter of fact," said Brian. "We're on our way to Pillow Mountains."

Fred and Freda looked at each other.

"There's nothing wrong in going to Pillow Mountains, is there?" asked Paul. "We told the Blankets that we were going there."

"Oh you know Pure and Top Blanket then, do you?" asked Freda.

"Yes," said Paul. "We've just been to the circus with them."

"Oh dear, oh dear," said Freda. "The two of you must be very important people then."

"No, not really," said Paul. "We're just on a visit to Blanketland."

"An official visit?" asked Fred.

Paul wasn't sure what that meant but Brian understood what Fred had asked.

Quickly he answered him. "No, not an official visit. It's a private visit. We just decided to come and here we are."

Freda was looking very carefully at Paul and Brian. "Here you are from where?" she asked.

"From the other side of Blanketland," said Brian.

"The other side?" said Freda. "I've never heard of the other side of Blanketland. Are you sure you haven't been sent here to find out things?"

"What kind of things?" asked Paul.

"Well, about the feather harvest," said Fred, who by now was as worried as Freda.

"So those are feathers that are growing in the fields," said Paul.

"Well, what would you expect to be growing at Feather Farm?" asked Fred.

"I don't know," said Paul. "It's just that Brian and I have never seen feathers growing before. What do you use them for?"

"For the Pillow Mountains, of course," said Fred. "What do you think we use them for?"

"But surely the Pillow Mountains are

full of feathers already," said Brian.

"They get flattened and worn out," said Fred.

Then, seeing that Brian and Paul didn't understand, he added "By the skiers."

"The skiers?" Brian and Paul both said the words at the same time.

"Yes, of course. Don't tell me they don't have skiers on the mountains on the other side of Blanketland."

"Yes, of course they do," said Paul. "But there they ski on snow."

"Snow?" said Freda. "What's snow?"

"Well it's soft white stuff," said Paul.

"Sounds like cream that you get from milk," said Freda.

As soon as she said the work milk all the cows, who had been standing around very quietly, started to bounce up and down. They also began to once more shout "Klim! Klim! Klim!"

"Now look what you've done," said Fred to Freda. "You've made the cows nervous."

"Then you'd better take care of them," said Freda.

Fred clapped his hands and said to the cows: "Line up. You all know your places."

The cows at once stopped bouncing around and lined up close to the yellow and green shed.

Fred went inside the shed and came out with a long blue hose-pipe in his hand.

The first cow opened her mouth.

Fred turned the hose pipe on.

A stream of milk came out.

When the cow had enough milk she bounced to the other side of the farmyard. This time she called out "Milk! Milk! Milk!"

The same thing happened with all the other cows.

Then Fred went back into the shed with the hose-pipe.

Brian and Paul were amazed.

Paul said, "On our farm we usually get milk FROM the cows instead of giving it to them."

Freda said: "I've never heard anything so strange in my entire life."

Brian said: "Of course, these aren't really cows."

"Aren't really cows?" Fred came out of the shed and slammed the door. "What are they then?"

"Well they are more like the jugs that Paul's granny collects," said Brian.

"Jugs?" said Freda "How can they be jugs if they aren't made of blanket?"

"I don't know," said Paul, "but they most certainly aren't real cows. And if everything in Blanketland is made of blanket, how is it that the cows aren't made of blanket?"

"What are they made of then?" asked Fred.

"They are made of china. Touch them and you'll see," said Brian.

"China? Are you sure?" asked Freda.

"Yes, I'm absolutely certain," said Brian. "If they weren't made of china the milk would spill."

"Where does the milk come from?" asked Paul.

"Why, from the milk lake," said Fred. "Underneath this farm there is a thick layer of mattress. Under the mattress is the great milk lake."

"And where do the cows go with the milk?" asked Paul.

"Why to the great milk river," said Freda. "It's on the edge of Blanketland."

"And what happens to it there?" asked Paul.

"The cows empty the milk into it. It flows all the way under Blanketland and back into the lake," said Fred.

"But wouldn't it be easier to just leave it in the lake?" asked Brian.

"The lake might overflow," said Freda.

"But if it's under the ground what difference could that make?" asked Paul.

"It might damage the Pillow Mountains," said Freda. "And anyway what would the cows do all day long if they didn't carry the milk from the lake to the river?"

"They could just be jugs," said Paul.

The cows began to bounce higher and higher off the ground. They all shouted the word "Milk! Milk! Milk!"

"If they are not careful," said Brian "they will turn that milk sour."

The word "sour" made the cows twice as

cross. They bounced even higher and began to bump into each other.

"They'll end up cracked, if they aren't careful," warned Paul.

"And whose fault will that be?" asked Freda. "Yours and Brian's for coming here uninvited and upsetting everyone."

"But the notice down at the gate said 'Afternoon Tea. Bed and Breakfast.' You must get a lot of people who come here without being invited," replied Paul.

"Yes, but they don't upset the cows," said Freda.

"We didn't mean to upset the cows," said Paul. "We just wondered what was going on."

"Oh, so you *were* sent here then to find out about things," said Fred.

"No, no, no. We followed the cows to see if we could find anyone who could tell us a short cut to Pillow Mountains."

"A short cut?" Fred and Freda looked at each other again.

As for the cows they stopped bouncing for a second, rolled their eyes in fright and then bounced out of the farmyard and back down the road.

"Now what have we done?" asked Paul.

"You used the word that the inhabitants of Blanketland most hate to hear. You said 'cut'," replied Freda. "Can you imagine what happens to a blanket if you cut it?"

"It unravels," said Paul.

"Exactly," said Freda. "Now I think we should all have some tea. I know you and Brian said you didn't want any but, all the same, I think you should have some."

"That's very good of you," said Brian. "But we don't really have time. You see, Pure and Top said we'd have to hurry if we were to get to the mountains before dark."

"It will be dark in ten seconds," said Fred.

"But it's the middle of the afternoon," said Paul "How could it be dark in ten seconds?"

"Count to ten and you'll find out," said Freda.

Brian and Paul counted slowly to ten. As soon as they'd finished, the sun and the blue sky vanished.

In their place was a bright orange moon and a dark sky full of stars.

"There you are," said Fred. "What did I tell you?"

"And, of course, it's now far too late for tea," said Freda. "We'll all have to have supper."

She lead the way back into the house.

"The price of supper is twenty nine and a half tickles," said Fred.

"I've never heard of half-a-tickle," said Paul. "In fact I've never heard of anyone charging tickles for anything."

"But what else would you be charged in Blanketland?" asked Fred. "The place is run on tickles."

"Do please sit down," said Freda, pointing to a sofa.

Brian and Paul did as they were told.

The sofa turned out to be even softer than the road outside the house.

In fact it was so soft that Brian and Paul sank right down into it. Only their heads could be seen.

But neither Fred or Freda seemed to

notice what had happened.

"Maybe they are just being polite," Paul whispered to Brian. "I never thought blankets could be so soft."

"It's not blanket," said Brian. "It's feathers. The sofa is made of feathers. In fact everything in the room is made of feathers."

"Why so it is," said Paul, looking carefully around. "Even the curtains and the carpet. I wonder if we are still in Blanketland?"

"Oh yes, I think we are still in Blanketland," said Brian. "I think the reason it suddenly got dark was because the cows bouncing along made the blankets lift up and fall down over the farm."

"Do you mean like the way that blankets can fall on top of a pillow when a bed is made?" asked Paul.

Brian nodded. "Something else. I think Fred and Freda might be made of feathers as well."

"Would that make them nervous?"

"Well, feathers do flutter," said Brian.

"but we'd better stop whispering in case they start thinking again that we are spies sent by the Blankets."

"Yes, of course," agreed Paul. He looked around, trying to think of something to say.

Fred and Freda were standing in the middle of the room, watching him.

"How often do the cows come here to collect the milk?" he finally decided to say.

"Why would you want to know that?" asked Fred.

"I don't know," said Paul, trying to rise up a little out of the sofa.

A huge feather came loose and fluttered past his nose. It made his nose wriggle.

"Oh, I think I'm going to sneeze," said Paul "and I don't know if I have a handkerchief."

He tried to put his hand in the pocket of his pyjamas.

But all he managed to do was to make more feathers flutter and float in the air.

Brian's nose began to feel ticklish as well.

He tried to stop it from tickling.

Freda said in a very frightened voice: "Neither of you must sneeze! Whatever happens neither of you must sneeze. It could be worse than a cut."

"Indeed it could," agreed Fred. "A sneeze on Feather Farm could be much worse than a cut to a blanket."

But it was just too late because, before Paul found his handkerchief or Brian could stop his nose tickling, they both sneezed the biggest sneezes they had ever sneezed in their lives.

"AshOOOOO," went Brian.

"Ashoooo...ASHOOOOO," went Paul.

The air around them filled with feathers.

The sofa beneath them seemed to just vanish.

So too did the walls of the room.

It was as though Paul and Brian were in the middle of a great snowstorm.

"We've blown everything away," shouted Brian. "In fact I think we've blown ourselves up into the sky."

Paul pushed the feathers out of the

way.

Brian was right.

They were both high in the sky floating in a cloud of feathers.

The moon and the stars and the darkness had gone.

"Do you think we have sneezed ourselves into to-morrow?" asked Paul.

"No," said Brian. "I think we have sneezed the blankets back off Feather Farm. It's the middle of the afternoon again."

And so it was. The sun was once more shining out of a bright blue sky.

And the cloud of feathers was carrying Paul and Brian down, down to earth.

"Fred and Freda will be very cross with us," said Paul.

"I don't think we are going back to Feather Farm," said Brian. "I think that our sneezes have carried us all the way to Pillow Mountains."

"In other words the Feathers, without meaning to, have shown us the quickest short cut of all," laughed Paul.

"Exactly," said Brian.

They both closed their eyes.

Being carried along so gently on the cloud of feathers was like a wonderful warm dream.

With the gentlest of bumps they felt themselves land on soft, crunchy ground.

They opened their eyes.

They were on top of Pillow Mountains.

4

Pillow Mountains

 rian and Paul brushed the feathers off their clothes and looked around.

From where they stood they could see right across the creases and folds of Blanketland to where the big circus tent was.

They could see the herd of china cows bouncing along the winding road.

They could see the fields of feathers and the yellow and green shed. But where the farmhouse had been there was only a small pile of feathers.

"Oh dear," said Brian. "We seem to have ruined the farmhouse with our sneezing. I wonder what has happened to Fred and

Freda?"

He had no sooner spoken than a second cloud of feathers drifted down out of the sky.

In the middle of it were Fred and Freda.

They both looked very cross and started to shout as soon as they saw Brian and Paul.

"Oh so this is where you are, is it?"

"Thought you'd get away, did you?"

"Who is going to rebuild our farmhouse then?"

"Please," said Paul, "Brian and I don't know anything about building houses out of feathers."

"We could maybe build you one out of wood," said Brian.

"Out of wood?" Freda said, "I've never heard of such a thing, never!"

"Well, if you don't like wood we could maybe make you one out of stone," said Brian.

"Stone?" said Fred. "A house built of stones? And what would happen if the cows bumped into it? They'd be broken into bits."

"Well, blankets then," said Brian. "I have a needle and thread. Like all leprechauns I'm very good at sewing. All we would have to do is find some blankets and cut them up in squares."

"Cut blankets up into squares!" said Freda. "Why the very idea! Not only is that not allowed but, if we let you do it, no one in Blanketland would ever talk to us again. Are you quite sure you are friends of Top and Pure Blanket?"

"Yes, of course we are," said Paul.

"Well, I think they would be very cross if they heard you and Brian talking about cutting up blankets."

"We were only trying to help," said Paul.

"Well if that is your idea of help, we are better off managing by ourselves. Come along, Fred," said Freda.

"Oh, please, don't go away cross," said Paul.

But Fred and Freda had decided not to listen to another word. They bent their knees and called out "Ski! Ski!"

Then they sped off down the mountain

back to Feather Farm.

"They are skiing without skis," said Paul.

"Well anything is possible on mountains made of pillows," said Brian. "Why don't you and I try it? But let's go as far away as we can from Feather Farm. We seem to cause trouble there."

Brian and Paul turned their back on Feather Farm. They bent their knees like Fred and Freda had. They shouted out "Ski! Ski!"

Suddenly they were skiing down the mountain.

"It's the mountain that's moving," Brian called out.

"So it is," said Paul looking down at the ground beneath his feet. It was moving quickly like an escalator.

"I wonder how we stop," said Brian.

"Why do you want to stop?" asked Paul.

"Because of that," said Brian.

Straight ahead of them was what looked like the edge of a snow covered cliff.

"What happens when we get to that?"

asked Brian.

"Maybe if we were to call out 'stop ski' the ground might stop moving," Paul said.

They called out "Stop ski, Stop ski!" But the ground continued to move quickly under their feet.

"Maybe we should try calling 'Ski' backwards like the cows did with the word 'milk'."

"And what's 'ski' backwards?" asked Brian. "We are moving so fast that I can hardly think."

"Ski backwards is 'Isk'," replied Paul.

But before they could try calling out "isk, isk," they had reached the edge of the cliff and gone way over it!

Now, instead of skiing without skis, they were flying without wings.

Down below them was a wonderful valley with crowds of people and rows and rows of coloured flags. The sound of cheering could be heard.

"I think they must be cheering us," said Brian.

"I just hope we don't land on anybody," said Paul. "I wish we had another cloud of

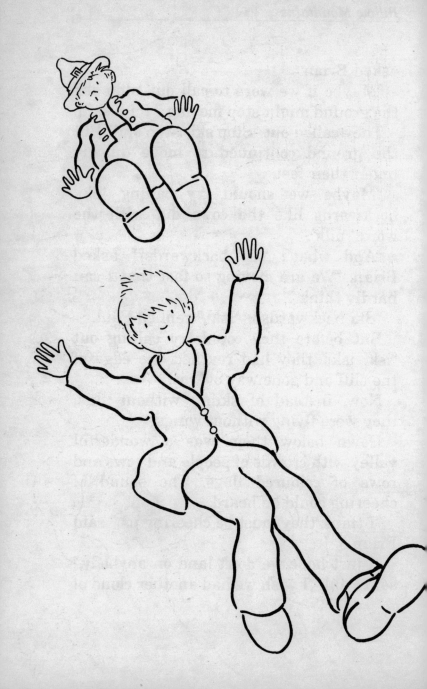

feathers to help us."

But they had no need for a cloud of feathers.

They began to come slowly and gently down out of the sky.

They landed where the first row of flags was and skid easily along.

They finally came to a stop where the first of the people stood.

A big red-faced man stepped forward. "Well done," he said "Well done! I have never seen a jump like that. You've won first prize in the Pillow Mountain Ski Jump Contest. Here are your gold medals."

While all the people standing around cheered and cheered, the man pinned one gold medal on Paul and another one on Brian.

"But it's all a mistake," said Paul. "We didn't know there was a contest."

"You didn't know there was a contest and still you made that jump!" The man shook hands with Paul and Brian. "Why that makes it even better! You must do it again! In fact you must teach all of us how to jump!"

"Well, we're very tired right now," said Brian.

"And cold," said Paul.

In spite of the bright sunshine it was not as warm as might be expected in the valley. Also, of course, his pyjamas were not very suitable for skiing and jumping.

"In fact I wouldn't mind getting away from here," said Paul.

"Get away?" said the man.

"Oh I don't mean that it isn't very nice here. It is nice; one of the nicest places I've ever seen. But you see, I've been sick in bed," explained Paul.

"Oh then you must go to the hospital," the man said.

"No, no. There's no need for that," said Brian.

"It's no trouble to arrange it," said the man. "In fact we have an ambulance right here in case of accident."

The crowd stood back.

Paul and Brian saw a bright orange ambulance with two men standing beside it, wearing pale grey uniforms.

"Take our two medal winners to the hospital at once!"

The two ambulance men hurried forward, carrying a stretcher.

Brian said: "We do not need to go to the hospital."

"No," said Paul, "but I need to get away from here before I freeze. They won't keep us in the hospital when they see that we are not very sick."

The two ambulance men put the stretcher down on the ground.

It was wide enough for both Brian and Paul to lie on it.

The ambulance men covered them with blankets.

Then they tried to lift the stretcher. But it was too heavy with Paul and Brian on it.

Several people from the crowd offered to help.

After much heaving and panting they managed, at last, to lift the stretcher.

In spite of the extra help the ambulance men still almost dropped Brian and Paul.

"This is almost as dangerous as the

jump," said Paul. "I had no idea we were so heavy."

"It's not that we are heavy," said Brian. "It's just that they are so light."

"Light?" said Paul. "Do you mean they are made of feathers?"

"More likely out of pillow cases, only don't let them hear us talking like this. They might start to wonder what we are made of."

Fortunately at that moment they reached the back of the ambulance.

The ambulance men and their helpers tried to put the stretcher gently inside. But they tilted the stretcher too much. Paul and Brian rolled out onto the floor.

No one else seemed to mind. Or maybe they were so happy to get the stretcher as far as the ambulance that they didn't notice what had happened.

The back doors of the ambulance were closed.

The two ambulance men got into the front seats.

With a great wailing siren they drove off as if the ambulance was part of a race.

It skidded around corners.

It bumped over lumps.

It ran down into hollows.

Every time Brian and Paul tried to stand up they fell back down.

At last the ambulance screeched to a stop.

The back doors were opened.

Several doctors and nurses looked in at Brian and Paul, lying flat on the floor with the stretcher on top of them.

"This looks a very serious case of upside-down," said the oldest of the doctors. "They must be put on a diet of thread and milk for the next seventy-five years!"

"But there is nothing seriously wrong with us," said Paul, pushing the stretcher away and standing up.

"That's right," said Brian "and anyway we can't stay here for seventy-five years, eating thread and milk!"

"You must do as you are told," a nurse said sweetly. "Our hospital is the best there is."

"Maybe so, but it is not for us," said

Brian.

He and Paul jumped down out of the ambulance.

The ground beneath their feet gave a loud ripping noise.

A great tear appeared in it.

The nurses and the doctors all backed away.

"Come on," said Brian, "now is our chance."

He jumped down into the tear.

Paul followed him.

5

The Mattress

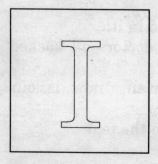t seemed to be only a few inches from the outside of the hospital to where Paul and Brian landed.

Yet nothing could be more different from Pillow Mountains than the place in which they now found themselves.

For one thing it was much, much warmer.

And flatter, with strange looking bushes growing.

There were also lines everywhere that divided the place into squares.

"Where are we?" asked Paul.

"We are under the Pillow Mountains and under the sheet. That tear that we jumped through was in the sheet."

"Under the Pillow Mountains and under the sheet," said Paul. "That must mean that we are on the mattress."

"Of course," said Brian. "That's exactly where we are. Most mattresses have lines like this."

"But do they have strange looking bushes growing on them?" asked Paul.

"They have funny things like flat buttons sewn onto them," said Brian. "That's what those bushes are."

"But why is it so warm?" asked Paul.

"I think it must be a desert," said Brian. "It looks like a dry, flat place."

"But what are we going to do here?" asked Paul. "We can't walk across a desert without any water to drink. Supposing we get lost?"

At that very moment they heard a strange sound.

It was half-way between a cough and a bark.

They turned around.

Coming very slowly towards them were two camels.

"Oh look," one of them said. "Strangers!

Where have you two come from then?"

"From Pillow Mountains," Brian said.

"Oh really," the camel said. "Did they try and put you in the hospital?"

"Yes," said Brian "they did."

"They try to do that with most people," said the camel.

"And do most people escape like we did?" asked Paul.

"Only the lucky ones," said the camel. "We've heard of several people who've been on a diet of thread and milk for years and years and years. But where are the two of you going?"

"We don't rightly know," said Brian. "We didn't really expect to be here at all."

"Well, you can go in four directions," the camel said. "You can go straight ahead or you can turn around and go back. Or you can go to the left. Or you can go to the right."

"Which way would you yourself think is best?" asked Brian.

"Well," said the camel, "we were going straight ahead."

"Then we'll go that way too," said Brian.

"Grand," said the camel. "We'll give you a lift."

"This'll be the second lift we've had today," Paul said. "Top and Pure Blanket took us to the circus in their carriage."

"Don't even talk to us about those Blankets," said the camel. "It's because of them that this place is so hot. They never think of anyone but themselves."

"But if you didn't have Blanketland up above you would the mattress not be too cold for camels?" asked Paul.

"Of course it wouldn't," said the camel. "It would be perfect."

The two camels knelt down. Brian and Paul scrambled up on their backs.

Brian was on the camel who had done all the talking.

Paul's camel seemed quite shy. It smiled very nicely however.

Brian said: "I think we should introduce ourselves. I'm Brian, the Leprechaun. I'm a travel agent. This is Paul, who goes to school."

"How very interesting," said the talkative camel. "My name is Hump. And

her name is Sandy."

"Oh so you're a lady camel," Paul said to his camel.

"That's right," Sandy said in a low, sweet voice. "Hump and I are going to a big party at the oasis."

"What's an oasis?" asked Paul.

"It's a wonderful place in the middle of the desert where trees grow and there is a lovely deep pool," said Hump. "There will be nice things to eat as well."

"Such as what?" asked Paul, who, suddenly, was very hungry.

"Date cakes and date sandwiches and date salad and date ice-cream," said Hump.

"Or you could have dates just by themselves," said Sandy.

"How interesting," Paul said politely.

He didn't in fact care very much for dates but thought it was rude to say so.

After a while he forgot about food altogether.

Riding on the camel was like being in a row-boat on a rough sea.

The camels swayed from side to side as

they moved along.

Soon Paul began to feel sea-sick.

He looked at Brian.

Brian had his eyes tightly closed. He looked very pale.

"He's feeling sick too," thought Paul. Then he closed his eyes.

That made him feel better.

After what seemed like an hour, Hump said: "We are almost there."

Paul and Brian opened their eyes.

Straight ahead of them was a huge circle of trees rising up out of the desert.

Lying in the shade of the trees were camels of all colours and sizes.

They began to call out to Sandy and Hump.

Sandy and Hump called back.

All the camels were very interested in Paul and Brian.

They offered them all kinds of date food.

Brian said: "I think we need a nice cool drink before we eat."

Hump said: "You must go to the pool."

He and Sandy knelt down to allow Brian and Paul to slide down to the ground.

Brian and Paul hurried forward to the centre of the oasis.

There was a pool there just like Hump had said. But, instead of being full of lovely clear water, the water was all grey and cloudy.

"I don't care much for the look of this water," said Brian.

"Neither do I," said Paul.

"I wonder if it got mixed up with the milk at the Feather Farm," said Brian.

"It looks to me like soapy water," said Paul. "It's the same colour as the water in the hand basin after I've washed my hands."

Brian dipped a finger in the pool and then tasted it.

He made a face.

"You're right," he said. "It is soapy water. We can't drink that."

"What's that there beside you?" asked Paul. "It looks like a chain."

"So it is," said Brian, giving the chain a pull.

There was a loud POP! from the middle

of the pool.

Bubbles began to appear.

The soapy water began to swirl around.

Within ten seconds all the water was gone out of the pool.

In the centre of the pool at the end of the chain there was a large white plug.

"We've pulled out the plug that kept the water in the pool," said Paul. "What will the camels say?"

The camels, hearing the sound of the water gurgling out of the pool, all hurried forward.

When they saw what had happened they were delighted.

"But there's no water now," said Paul. "And soapy water is better than none."

"You don't understand," said Hump. "We've been trying for years to get the plug out but could never manage it. Now we are entitled to a fresh supply."

"A fresh supply of water?" asked Brian.

"No," said Hump. "Of milk from Feather Farm. Fred and Freda refused to let us have any until the pool was empty."

"But how will it get here?" asked Paul.

"It'll come from under the desert," said Hump.

Hump had no sooner spoken than a new gurgling sound was heard.

This time it came from under the ground.

Milk began to bubble up through the floor of the pool.

"Should we not put the plug in soon?" asked Paul.

"No, no," said Hump. "That was the mistake we made the first time. If we hadn't put the plug in, the water could not have got all grey and soapy."

"And by leaving the plug out you will always have a supply of milk from Feather Farm," said Brian.

"Quite right," said Hump.

"But do camels drink milk?" asked Paul.

Hump looked worried. "I don't know," he said. "In fact I don't think we have ever had the chance to find out before now."

"Might it not be as well to taste it before any more comes out of the ground?" asked Brian.

Hump bent his head and tasted the milk.

He made a face like Brian had when he tasted the soapy water.

"Oh no," he said. "I don't like that very much. It tastes of feathers. Where's the plug? We have to stop the pool from getting full of such stuff."

But the plug and chain were hidden from sight underneath the milk.

"I suppose I could dive in and get it," said Paul. "But what good would that do? You would only end up with a pool full of sour milk."

"An oasis of sour milk might be more like it," said Hump as the milk reached the top of the pool.

It began to spread out onto the ground.

Brian and Paul and all the camels began to back away.

"We'll have to go back to Feather Farm and ask them to turn off the supply," said Paul.

"Fred and Freda might not be too happy to see us," said Brian.

"That's a chance we will just have to

take," said Paul.

They climbed back up on Hump and Sandy.

The two camels galloped across the desert, followed by all the other camels.

Paul kept his eyes open. He looked back at the oasis.

The milk was flowing out of it, covering the desert.

Ahead of them they could see the hole in the sheet.

"You will have to try to jump up through it," said Brian to Hump.

"Right," said Hump. "Hold on tight."

Together he and Sandy jumped right up through the hole and landed at the foot of the Pillow Mountains.

There was no sign of the hospital or the ambulance or any of the people.

"Everyone's gone," said Brian.

"And it'll take ages to get back across the mountains," said Paul.

"Maybe if we were to shake the mountains," said Brian.

He rushed forward and began to push at the mountains. They moved quite easily.

Paul and Hump and Sandy joined in.

So did the rest of the camels as they jumped up through the hole.

Soon they had pushed the Pillow Mountains to one side.

There, in front of them, was Feather Farm.

The farmhouse had been rebuilt. It looked better than ever.

Fred and Freda were standing in the farmyard.

"What's happening?" asked Fred.

"Who pushed the mountains to one side?" asked Freda.

"We did," said Paul.

"I might have known it would be the two of you. What are the camels doing here?"

"They came with us from the desert. The oasis is flooded with milk," said Brian.

Fred rushed into the shed.

There was the sound of a handle being turned.

Then he came back out.

"I've switched the milk off," he said. "Everything should be alright."

"But what about the milk in the pool?" asked Paul.

"Oh that'll soon drain away," said Fred.

"And what will happen then?" asked Brian. "You can't leave the pool empty."

Fred wrinkled his brow. "I suppose you could have water if you liked."

"But fresh water," said Paul.

"Of course," said Fred. "The camels can carry it in their humps like the cows carry the milk."

"And where will the water come from?" asked Brian.

"Why from the rain barrel outside the window," said Freda.

"Outside what window?" asked Paul.

"Outside your window, of course," said Brian. "Did you forget how this adventure started?"

"Yes, I did" said Paul.

"Well while everything seems to be alright here, maybe we should count to three again and jump," said Brian.

Paul closed his eyes and counted to

three.

When he opened them again he was back in his own bed.

Brian was sitting on the edge of the dressing table.

"The gold medals are gone," said Paul.

"They must have fallen off when we jumped down into the mattress desert," said Brian. "But you know how to get back to Blanketland if you want to look for them. Just count to three. Now I think I can hear your mother coming upstairs."

Paul's mother opened the door of the bedroom. She was carrying a tray. On it was a bowl of delicious soup almost the colour of the feather milk, and a plate of brown bread and butter.

"Well you had a nice, long sleep this morning," she said. "I looked in earlier on. You didn't even hear me. Do you think you could manage to eat this?"

"Oh yes. I'm sure I could." Paul felt even hungrier now that he was back from Blanketland.

Brian slipped out of the bedroom and back to the bathroom window.

Bríd, the blackbird, was waiting there for him.

"You've no need to worry anymore about Paul," said Brian. "He'll get better now that he knows how to get to Blanketland. It's time I got back to the travel agency."

While Bríd carried Brian back to the oak tree, Paul ate his soup.

He wished that Brian had been able to stay longer. But he knew that he would not be lonely any longer.

"And just wait until I tell them all at school," he said to himself.

Also by Tony Hickey in Children's Poolbeg

Joe in the Middle
Where is Joe?

Spike and the Professor
Spike and the Professor at the Races
Spike, the Professor and Doreen
Go to London

Foodland
Legendland

Joe in the Middle

by Tony Hickey

"A deep absorbing story"

Sunday Press

"An exciting and complicated tale,"

Books Ireland

POOLBEG

Where is Joe

by Tony Hickey

The exciting action-packed sequel to
Joe in the Middle

Children's
POOLBEG

Spike and the Professor

by Tony Hickey

A day of hilarious and disastrous
adventures for two friends who live
in Dublin

POOLBEG

Spike and the Professor and Doreen at the Races

by Tony Hickey

The accident-prone duo get together with Spike's sister, Doreen and the highly original Brunhilde Brisk for even more hair-raising adventures at the races.

Children's
POOLBEG